Apple Pie Press
Publishing
P.O. Box 695
Farmington, Utah 84025

TICKLE·KINGDOM

Robert D. Harris
c/o Apple Pie Press
P.O. Box 695
Farmington, Utah 84025

The paintings in this book were done in watercolor and color pencil.
The text type was set in Times New Roman

Book manufactured by Hiller Industries
Salt Lake City, Utah

Printed in the United States of America
First Edition

ISBN: 1-56713-122-0
Library of Congress Catalog Card Number: Applied for.

heh-heh

cock-a-doodle-doo!

To my eight children who make
storytelling fun and life a blast.

– Robert Harris

To Alex, Joshua and Jacob.
Daddy, I wish you were here.

– Maren Scott

"If you want your children to be brilliant tell them fairy tales. If you want them to be very brilliant, tell them even more fairy tales."
– Albert Einstein

TICKLE KINGDOM

by
Robert D. Harris

Illustrated by
Maren J. Scott

LONG, long ago and far, far away, skies were still blue, waters were clear and large castles rose majestically throughout the countryside. Kings and Queens sat and sprawled in spacious splendor and poor peasants prepared potato porridge.

But a deep sadness filled the land. No one smiled. No one laughed. No one celebrated. No, not so much as an old man's snicker or a child's heartwarming laugh had been heard for over ten long years.

Down in the village, in their humble cottage, Hans and Ruth hurried up the small wooden ladder that led from the kitchen to their loft. They snuggled down into their straw bed and pulled the warm, wool blanket mother had knitted right up under their chins. Tomorrow would be the most exciting day of their lives. Hans and Ruth were going to the castle with their father. They tried to fall asleep quickly so tomorrow would come. The warm August wind whistled through the thatched roof, but tonight it didn't frighten Hans and Ruth. It only made them fall asleep faster.

Early each day before school and again just before dark, Hans and Ruth milked the three cows. And all day long Mr. and Mrs. Smitt worked fast and hard making butter and cheese. People came from near and far to buy it. Everyone said the Smitt's butter and cheese was the most delicious in the whole land. Bessy, Bossie and Beatrice, the Smitt's prized cows, had been fed extra oats tonight for they had done their job well.

King Marcus and Queen Martha lived in the large castle on the hill, high above the Smitts' small cottage. They would eat nothing but the very best. When they heard of the Smitts' butter and cheese, they insisted they have some. So, the castle's chief cook, Conrad, sent a messenger with a large, urgent order to the Smitts.

The Smitts wasted no time in making the finest butter and cheese they had ever made. Now, as the sun set, the tired Smitts slept.

When the first rooster crowed, Hans and Ruth sprang out of bed dancing with excitement as they dressed.

In the rush, breakfast was almost missed, but Mrs. Smitt wrapped apples and cheese and biscuits in a soft green cloth and tied it with a piece of red yarn. The children would eat on the way to the castle. Carefully, they placed the large jars and buckets of cheese and butter in the back of the wagon and surrounded them with clean straw.

Nathaniel, their old but dependable horse, was hitched to the wooden wagon. Swinging his tail at a pesky fly and taking a long deep breath of cool morning air, Nathaniel leaned into his harness. The wagon rumbled slowly down the lane away from the small white cottage. Hans and Ruth sat on the back of the wagon dangling their bare feet and waving goodby. Mrs. Smitt stood in the doorway holding a baby in each arm as she called to Ruth, "Take care of Hans, and remember, don't let him laugh or smile!"

The morning
sun felt good
as it warmed
their skin. Ruth
made squiggly
designs in the cool
dust as she dragged her
bare feet. Hans pouted
because his feet didn't reach.
He was a few years younger
than Ruth, but he was not afraid of anything.

As they passed through the village, everyone greeted them the same way
— a simple "hello," no smiles, no good mornings.

The closer they came to the castle, the larger it appeared and the greater
their excitement became. Few peasants from the village had ever been
inside the castle walls.

The wagon jerked to a stop. Nathaniel snorted as a loud clanging broke the morning silence. The castle bridge clattered and creaked as it was slowly lowered across the moat. With hollow, clapping strides Nathaniel cautiously led the wagon with the cheese and the butter, the children and their father into the courtyard.

Guards, dressed in grey and white, with large silver swords, looked like toys against the grey, stone walls that rose almost to the clouds.

"Stay in the wagon," Mr. Smitt whispered to Hans and Ruth.
Fat little men and women in white uniforms with funny,
puffy hats scurried inside with the creamy
delicacies. Mr. Smitt followed them on
down to the cellar where it was cool.

Silence soon filled the courtyard. Hans and Ruth gazed in amazement at this new and unusual world from the back of the wagon. Then it happened. A mouse that had been hiding in the straw made his escape from the wagon.

He darted from the straw looking for safety in a large row of bushes. He ran across Hans' lap, over his knee and down his leg. Startled, Hans jumped and kicked just as the mouse reached his foot.

The mouse tumbled higher and higher into the air. High enough, in fact, to land gracefully on top of the wall surrounding the castle. Ruth trembled, grabbed her mouth with one hand and pinched herself with the other. But she knew nothing could stop what was going to happen.

She laughed.

Not a loud laugh, but a shy, quiet whisper of a laugh.

A rumbling, gruff voice bellowed from above, "Who is laughing?" King Marcus had been basking in the early morning sun on a balcony above the courtyard.

"Bring me the person who laughed," demanded the King. Two guards, who had been so still that they simply looked like statues, sprang to life, sending chills down the children's backs.

With metal armor clanging against their sharp swords, they grabbed Ruth from the wagon. With each guard holding a pigtail, they dragged her up the winding, stone staircase to the balcony. Hans hid under the straw.

The short, fat King, who had a red face and curly blonde hair, was sitting on a big, green, velvet chair facing the simmering sun. The guards dropped Ruth at his feet. Dangling a bunch of red grapes, King Marcus chomped off a sloppy mouthful and began chewing.

The way he ate strangely reminded Ruth of her neighbor's pig.

With red juice dripping from the corners of his mouth, King Marcus bellowed, "How can such a pretty little girl be so stupid?"

"I'm not stupid! I'm quite smart!" snapped Ruth. "Then why did you laugh?" yelled the King. "What's wrong with laughing?" asked Ruth. "There's a law against it, that's what's wrong with it!" said the King.

"Well, it's a dumb law," said Ruth. "People want to laugh and smile and be happy. Why don't you let them?"

"Because it's my law. That's the way it has always been and that's the way it's going to stay," the King huffed.

Growing impatient, King Marcus turned to a tall, skinny man with a long, sad face who was holding a big, black book. The King asked, "What does it say will happen to someone who laughs?"

"Umm, uh . . . on page nine, uh, line, humm, seven, it says, uh . . ."

"Come on! Come on! What does it say?" shouted the angry King.

"Uh, it says, 'Five years in the dungeon for laughing'!"

"Then that's where you're going, little girl!" snapped the King.

"Guards! Guards! Take her away and lock her up!"

"You're a mean old King. You don't let anybody laugh or be happy and you eat like a PIG!" cried Ruth, as the guards grabbed her.

Hans heard everything that was happening and knew he had to help his sister. Jumping out of the wagon, he headed for the staircase that led to the balcony. But two guards clanged their swords together and sparks flew. The stairway was blocked!

Hans frantically looked around! The rough stone wall leading to the balcony was covered by a grapevine. Its twisted stems and large leaves blanketed the side of the castle. Hans looked like a little red haired monkey, with ears that were just a little too large, as he quickly climbed up, up, up through the cool green leaves. Grasping the top of the wall with one hand and a thick branch with the other, he poked his freckled face through the thick leaves and yelled, "STOP! Let my sister go!"

Startled, King Marcus jumped out of his chair knocking over a plant. Stumbling backwards, his eyes got bigger and bigger as he looked at the funny little boy.

"What do you want?" demanded the King.

"I want you to let my sister go," demanded Hans.

"Take them both to the dungeon," roared King Marcus as he turned to go inside.

Jumping from the balcony, Hans landed on the King's wide back. He buried his pink little fingers under the King's short, fat arms, and started to tickle. King Marcus began to wiggle. He jumped and jerked. He swung and swayed. He yelled and yakked. He bounced and bobbled.

But it did no good. The more he heaved and hopped, the harder Hans held. The faster the King thrashed and trod and threw, the more Hans tickled and tickled and tickled.

King Marcus resisted with all his might, but the sound started slowly and softly,
growing until it filled the balcony. King Marcus was laughing! Laughter filled
the balcony, spilling over the castle wall and into the courtyard. It rolled over
the bridge and drifted through the streets of the village. It became so loud and
so long and so lovely it filled the whole land!

The laughing King finally fell still. Hans dropped to the floor. Silence filled the air. The birds quit chirping. The leaves quit rustling. The servants stopped serving.

The Queen gasped. "Marcus, you laughed!"

"Yes," said the King, "for the first time in ten years, I have laughed!"

With tears flowing from his squinty little eyes, rolling over his round little cheeks and dropping onto the marble floor, Marcus the mighty King held Hans and Ruth in his arms. He then explained why he had made such a terrible law!

"Ten years ago I banned a wicked wizard from the kingdom. One night while everyone was sleeping, he returned to the castle. Finding my little boy and little girl asleep, he turned them to stone. I thought I could never be happy again. The Queen thought she could never be happy again. If we couldn't be happy, we thought no one should be happy," sobbed the King.

"So now what are you going to do?" asked the Queen. "You laughed, Marcus, and you broke the law."

With a grin on his face and a sparkle in his eye, King Marcus, the mighty magistrate, turned to the tall, skinny man with the large, black book and said, "Smile, Samuel!" And Samuel did.

"Record this new law on page nine, line seven," directed King Marcus. "From this day forth, everyone in the kingdom shall greet each other with either a laugh or a smile. Handshakes shall be allowed, but tickles preferred!"

Ruth decided that up close in his arms, the King really didn't look at all like the neighbor's pig.

Holding their hands, the King walked the children down the steps and placed them in the wagon. With an almost noticeable skip, he climbed back up the steps to the balcony.

Having completed his business with the cooks and helpers in the cellar, Mr. Smitt hurried to check on his children. They were both seated quietly in the wagon. "Have you children been behaving yourselves?" he asked.

"Of course, father," smiled the children.

King Marcus insisted the Smitts move to the castle. And they did. Mr. Smitt directed the dairy, Mrs. Smitt minded the nursery, and Hans and Ruth taught everyone in the kingdom how to laugh, smile and be happy. The King became the best tickler in Tickle Kingdom!

He He He He He He He He He He

Ha Ha Ha Ha Ha Ha Ha Ha Ha Ha Ha Ha Ha

And, so you see, a smile can be greater than the sword. Laughter lasts long after loneliness leaves.

And a tickle? Well, a tickle can change a kingdom.

And learning to love and laugh again . . . . .

. . . it can perform miracles!

"No time is more
precious and well
rewarded than those
few moments you
spend reading a story
to a child."

– *Robert D. Harris*